Micah And the Vase

A Child's Book on Honesty

Written by: Kimally Samuels

Illustrated by: Mehk Arshad

This book is lovingly dedicated to my mother, Adrianne "Micah" Brown and my father, Jerry Samuels.

Mom, you finally got siblings!!

Thank you both for ALWAYS believing in me!

To my littles who are the inspiration for writing this book: Jamie Jr. ("JJ"), Elijah, Paisley Joy ("Paiz Maze"), Patience, Lydia, and Grace.

With love to: Pierce, Jalisa, Azim, Anais, Anthony, Trinity, Cynthia "London", Toya, Kai, Jahve', Yeshua, Jahi, Jayvin, Leilani, Noel, and Rayelle.

Micah had been in her bedroom all morning watching television. She knew that she should have been doing her chores but decided to watch a new cartoon that everyone in her third-grade class was talking about. She hadn't seen the show and she felt so left out. She had to watch it.

Her plan was to watch all the episodes this weekend so that she could go to school and talk with her friends about it on Monday. She was so excited! It seemed to be a good show and it was so funny. She would forever be a fan of Marco the Bunny!!

Her mother knocked on her door. Micah barely heard her.

Her mother quickly entered the room, stood there for a moment, located the remote and turned the television off.

"Micah, this room is a mess! Why are you watching television?"

"Mom…" Micah said, feeling frustrated because her mother was in the room.

"Mom, I was just…"

Her mother stopped her mid-sentence.

"Micah, you know that you are not supposed to watch television until your room is clean and all your chores are done. Do your chores!"

Clean your room

"Mom can I finish watching this episode and then clean my room? Please mom, please!!"

"Micah, if you haven't completed your chores, you can't watch television. You know the rules!"

Her mother pointed to a dress and some shoes on the floor: "Put those up!"

"And vacuum the living room too."

Micah, laying on the bed slowly rolled off and stood up.

Put those up

"Micah, you must be more responsible. When you do not follow the rules, you teach your younger sisters not to follow the rules.

Your sisters and I are getting ready to go to their ballet class, but your father is going to be home and he will come and check on your progress. Get your chores done and then you can watch television."

Two little heads popped in the door, "Bye Micah!" said her twin sisters Kim and Kia.

"Bye Kim, Bye Kia," said Micah.

After her mother left, Micah turned the television back on and started watching the show again.

Micah lost sense of the time,

One episode,

Two episodes,

Three episodes.

She heard a knock at the door. Startled, she rolled off the bed and turned off the television.

Her father walked into the room, "Micah, I heard the television on. You know you should be cleaning this room and doing your chores."

He unplugged the television and took the remote with him.

Micah checked the time.

Where had the time gone?

She realized her mother would return soon, so she hurriedly started working.

She cleaned her room and put everything in order, then she went to the living room and started vacuuming.

While Micah was vacuuming, she wasn't paying attention and knocked over a large, beautiful vase.

It broke into several giant pieces.

"Oh, No!" Micah cried. "What have I done?"

She waited for a moment; it did not seem that her father heard her.

She thought, "What will I do?"

The vase was older than she was and very expensive; her father had gotten it for her mother for their anniversary.

She knew her mother loved it.

Out of desperation, Micah grabbed some glue and tried to glue the vase back together.

Gluing it together did not work, instead, it broke into more pieces.

And her fingers got stuck together!

Micah got scared and put the vase into a garbage bag and put it in her room under her bed.

She thought, "No one will notice the vase is missing."

Later, when her mother and twin sisters returned, Micah had cleaned her room and completed her chores. She was in her room reading a book when she heard Kim and Kia running through the house.

"Wow Micah, this house is really clean!" said the twins in unison.

Micah's mother agreed, "Well done, Micah."

"Thank you, Mommy," Micah said nervously.

For the rest of that night, Micah did everything her mother asked with no hesitation and no complaints.

She helped her mother set the table for dinner, she cleared the table without being asked, and she washed the dinner dishes.

Her mother asked, "Is everything okay, Micah?"

"Yes, Mommy," Micah replied.

Micah had a difficult time falling to sleep that night.

She laid in the bed looking at the ceiling. She felt guilty.

She knew that she needed to tell the truth, but she did not want to get in trouble.

She felt awful.

Eventually Micah fell asleep.

She started to dream.

In the dream her Father, Mother, Kim and Kia, were in her room asking Micah where the vase was; she said she did not know.

Then, suddenly, the bag with the broken pieces floated up from under the bed and she could hear people singing,

"Micah broke the vase!

Micah broke the vase!"

Her parents shook their heads in disappointment. Her mother started to cry, and Micah saw the word, LIAR flash several times in front of her. She felt distance between herself and her family.

This dream is a nightmare...

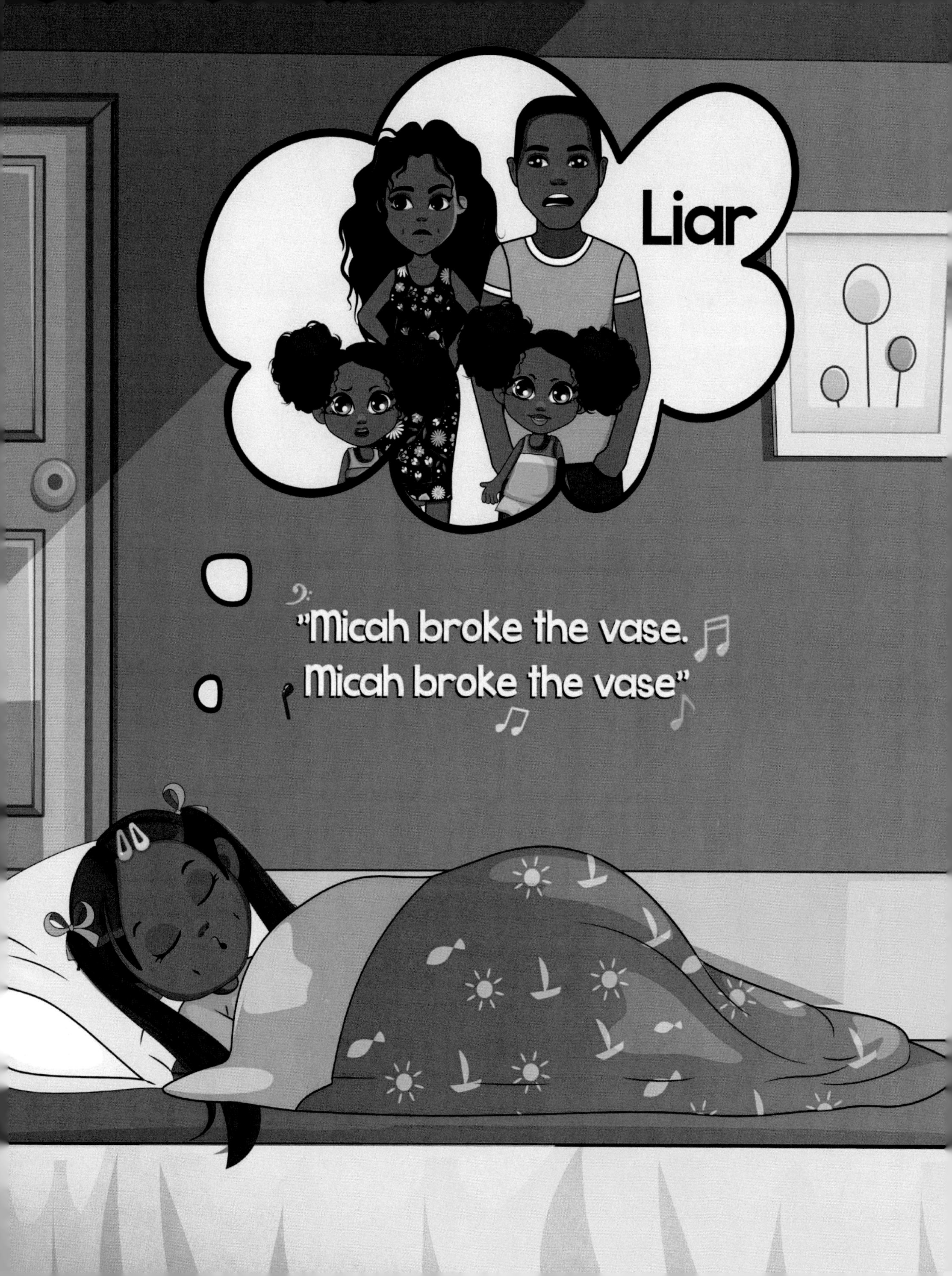
Liar
"Micah broke the vase.
Micah broke the vase"

When Micah woke up the next morning, she felt guilty and ashamed.

She checked under the bed and the bag with the broken vase was still there. Micah knew she had to make the situation right.

I have to make this right!

She went to her parent's room with the bag and the broken vase.

She explained to her parents that she was vacuuming, not paying attention and broke the vase. She admitted that she tried to put it back together and then hid it.

She apologized for her actions.

Micah's mother said, "I noticed the vase was missing when I got home yesterday."

Micah's parents thanked her for telling them the truth. They had a discussion with her about the importance of honesty. They explained that being honest is always best.

It was the first time Micah would learn the word "trustworthy". Her parents said that when you are honest people experience you as trustworthy. She did not completely understand what that meant, but she knew in time she would.

Honesty

Character

Truth

Integrity

Trustworthy

After the discussion, Micah's parents reminded her that they loved her. They both hugged and kissed her. They told her they were proud of her for telling the truth.

She was reminded that though she told the truth, there would be consequences because she had lied. Micah would not be able to play on her tablet or watch television for two weeks.

Micah was relieved to hear her punishment; not playing on a tablet and not watching television was nothing compared to the nightmare she had.

That night when Micah went to bed, she was comfortable, and she felt "light" and when she dreamed it was about unicorns. She slept like a baby.

THE END

Made in the USA
Columbia, SC
28 December 2022